Now, some of his friends had pets that suited them right down to the ground.

Little Miss Chatterbox had a parrot and she and her parrot chatted all day long and all night long.

Mr Quiet had a goldfish and they both lived very happily in silence.

And Mr Bounce had a kangaroo.

He did not take his kangaroo for a walk.

Oh no, he and his kangaroo went for a daily bounce.

Some of Mr Muddle's friends had pets that did not suit them at all.

Mr Sneeze owned a very fluffy cat, which made him sneeze.

Mr Worry had a tiger, which was not good for his nerves.

And Little Miss Quick had a tortoise.

And then some of Mr Muddle's friends had just got things all wrong.

Like Mr Topsy-Turvy who made a very topsy-turvy hutch for his rabbit.

Like Little Miss Scatterbrain who remembered to exercise her dog every day, but wasn't sure who was walking who.

And like Mr Wrong who thought he'd provided everything his hamster needed.

It had a cage with sawdust.

Food and water every day.

And a hamster wheel.

But for some reason the hamster wheel wouldn't go round!

Mr Muddle wanted to make sure that he picked just the right pet for himself, but he was all in a muddle.

There were so many pets to choose from at the pet shop.

He could not make up his mind.

It was Mr Nonsense who came to Mr Muddle's aid.

Mr Nonsense lived in Nonsenseland.

A place where the grass is blue and greenhouses are green.

Mr Nonsense had a pet.

A pet banana!

"You should get a puppy," suggested Mr Nonsense to Mr Muddle.

A puppy sounds like a very sensible suggestion doesn't it?

But how might a puppy suit Mr Muddle?

Mr Muddle followed Mr Nonsense's advice and bought a puppy for himself.

A very cute puppy.

A puppy with a tail that wagged.

A puppy with a cold wet nose.

A puppy that, when you rubbed its tummy, went …

… MOO!

It was a Nonsenseland puppy.

A muddled up Nonsenseland puppy.

And it suited Mr Muddle right down to the ground and all the way up to the sky.

Where a bird was flying by.

"Woof!" said the bird.